The Birthday Moon

By Lois Duncan
Pictures by Susan Davis

VIKING KESTREL

VIKING KESTREL
Published by the Penguin Group
Viking Penguin, a division of Penguin Books USA Inc.,
40 West 23rd Street, New York, New York 10010, U.S.A.
Penguin Books Ltd, 27 Wrights Lane, London W8 5TZ, England
Penguin Books Australia Ltd, Ringwood, Victoria, Australia
Penguin Books Canada Ltd, 2801 John Street, Markham, Ontario, Canada L3R 1B4
Penguin Books (N.Z.) Ltd, 182–190 Wairau Road, Auckland 10, New Zealand

Penguin Books Ltd, Registered Offices: Harmondsworth, Middlesex, England

First published in 1989 by Viking Penguin, a division of Penguin Books USA Inc.
1 3 5 7 9 10 8 6 4 2

Library of Congress Cataloging-in-Publication Data
Duncan, Lois Birthday moon
Lois Duncan ; pictures by Susan Davis. p. cm.
Summary: Relates the wonderful things you can do with the perfect
birthday gift—the moon.
ISBN 0-670-82238-8
[1. Moon—Fiction. 2. Birthdays—Fiction.] I. Davis, Susan,
1948– ill. II. Title.
PZ7.D9117Bi 1989 [E]—dc20 89-8989

Printed in Japan.

For my brother Bill
with love from his old friend
"Jack Moonshine"

L.D.

For Bob with whom I share the
best present of all, Love.

S.D.

On your very next birthday
I'll give you a moon

On the end of a string
Like a golden balloon.

You can tell all your friends
That it came from a shop.

Don't let anyone pinch it
And make it go "POP!"

I will give you a moon like a big yellow ball
You can hurl at the stars or can bounce off a wall.

You can bat it or kick it
Or toss it up high

So it flattens the clouds
As it rolls through the sky.

I will give you a moon
Like a coin you can spend.
You can buy yourself candy
To share with a friend.

You can spend it on stars
Or a comet's long tail,

Or you might buy the sun
If it's ever for sale.

If your birthday should come
When the moon is not whole,
I will give you a moon
You can use as a bowl.

You can fill it with cherries
Or ice cream or soup.
If you use it for parties
It serves quite a group.

I will give you a moon to be used as a bow
So the arrows you shoot will all shimmer and glow.

They will streak through the dark
Leaving highways of light

That the fireflies can take
If they're lost in the night.

You will not need a bed.
If you use a half-moon
As a hammock to doze in
Each warm afternoon.
It can hang from two branches
And swing in the breeze
While you're taking a nap
In the shade of the trees.

I will give you a half-moon
With spiderweb strings
You can pluck like a harp when
The nightingale sings.

Then your friends will all beg you
To play them some tunes,

For there's simply no music
As sweet as the moon's.

If you want to go fishing,
Just whisper to me
And I'll give you a half-moon
To sail on the sea.
You can throw out your nets
Where the star-minnows swarm,
And a moonship won't sink
If you're caught in a storm.

I will give you a half-moon
To wear on a chain,
Or to be an umbrella
To use in the rain,
Or to hold by a handle
And use for a spoon.
There are so many things
You can do with a moon!

When your moon's very tiny
And brittle and thin,
I will give you a box you
Can carry it in.
You must wrap it in cotton
And treat it with care
For a small moon is fragile
And easy to tear.

Was there ever a present
As fine as a moon?
Oh, I *do* hope your birthday
Is coming quite soon!